3
4
3
+4
7
6
9
10

For Timothy, Brian,

and Julie Stanton

ISBN 0-590-33614-2

12 11 10 9 8 7 6 5 4 3 2 1 9 5 6 7 8 9/8 0/9

Printed in the U.S.A. 10

NORMAN BRIDWELL

COUNT ON Clifford

SCHOLASTIC INC.

New York Toronto London Auckland Sydney

1

Hi! My name is Emily Elizabeth. This is my dog, Clifford. There is only **one** Clifford in all the world. Count **one** Clifford.

On Clifford's birthday, I gave him a party.

We were going to have a lot of balloons.
I blew up **two** balloons. Then I got tired.

Clifford tried to blow up the rest.
Clifford blew a little too hard, so we
just had two balloons. Count two balloons.
Count two girls. Count two boys.

I bought Clifford **three** presents. Count three presents. I wrapped them up. I was going to put bows on them.

But Clifford found the ribbons first.

What a mess!

Count three windows.

I invited Clifford's dog friends.

Four of them came. I didn't ask any cats.

Count four of Clifford's dog friends.

Count four houses. Count four party hats.

We played musical chairs. I set up **five** chairs.
Count five chairs. Count two yellow chairs.
Count three blue chairs.

We ran around and around.
When the music stopped,
Clifford was the first
to sit down. No more
musical chairs.

We played Hide-and-Seek. Clifford hid behind **six** trees. Count six trees.

We found Clifford anyway.

Then it was time for Clifford's cake. I put **seven** candles on the cake. Count seven candles. Count seven forks.

Clifford blew out the candles.

We had ice cream instead.

Clifford opened his gifts.

Everyone had the same idea.

Clifford got **eight** sacks of dog food.
Count eight sacks. Count four red sacks.
Count four yellow sacks.

9

We had a clown at the party.
The clown juggled **nine** balls.
Count nine balls. Count four red balls.
Count five yellow balls.

Clifford wanted to juggle, too.

Oops!

Then some cats came. They wanted to play games, too. We asked them to join us. They did. One, two, three, four, five, six, seven, eight, nine, ten.

Ten cats in all! Count ten cats. Count three gray cats. Count three white cats. Count four striped cats.

We were having fun.
Then I felt a raindrop.

Oh, no! It was raining.
The party would be ruined.

Count the children. Count the dogs. Don't forget to count Clifford.

But Clifford knew what to do. He saved the party. I always knew I could count on Clifford.

Count the boys. Count the girls.
Count the cats. Count the dogs.
Count the party hats.
HAPPY BIRTHDAY, CLIFFORD!

1
2
5
7
8